# The Judge Is Trapped—in a Hair-Raising Adventure!

I planned to just slip out when the door opened. I mean it was a ladies' room, and I was pretty embarrassed by the whole matter. But before I could ease out, the woman backed in! She shut the door, removed her glasses, and stepped to the sink to clean them.

She was drying those thick glasses. Bending down to set her briefcase on the floor, she met me nose to nose.

I was prepared to be friends until I heard, "*Eeeeeeeek!* Bear! Grizzly! *Eeeek!*"

Bear? I'd heard of mistaken identity, but this was ridiculous. If she would just put those glasses back on . . . so I nudged her hand.

"He's attacking! Help!"

"HILARIOUS . . . an inviting, accessible, and quickly read story. With humorous pencil drawings that delight."

—*ALA Booklist*

**Books by Judith Whitelock McInerney**

JUDGE BENJAMIN: SUPERDOG
JUDGE BENJAMIN: THE SUPERDOG SECRET

Available from ARCHWAY paperbacks

# JUDGE BENJAMIN: THE SUPERDOG SECRET

Judith Whitelock McInerney

Drawings by Leslie Morrill

AN ARCHWAY PAPERBACK
Published by POCKET BOOKS • NEW YORK

An Archway Paperback published by
POCKET BOOKS, a division of Simon & Schuster, Inc.
1230 Avenue of the Americas, New York, N.Y. 10020



Published by arrangement with Holiday House, Inc.
Library of Congress Catalog Card Number: 82-48752



ISBN: 0-671-50055-4

First Archway Paperback printing September, 1984

10 9 8 7 6 5 4 3 2



Cover design by Milton Charles

Printed in the U.S.A.

IL 4+

for MARGERY,
*who opened the door*

# Chapter 1

The sun woke me at 5:39.

It was Mother's Day in Decatur, Illinois, and the prime weather felt like a pat on the back.

I don't exactly qualify as a mother—my two hundred pounds of furry male self won't fool anybody—but I have done my share of mothering.

I'm Judge Benjamin, the O'Riley Saint Bernard.

Maggie was our real mother of the day, but as an assistant mother, I felt like celebrating, too. Helping Maggie and Tom keep track of the O'Riley children is a pawful—make that four paws full: Seth, Kathleen, Annie, and the newest O'Riley, Maura—but I love it.

My big job became bigger with the disastrous tornado of April 3. The O'Riley house, heavily damaged in the storm, was being rebuilt room by room. Linoleum rolls, bricks, and plasterboard were everywhere. We were living in a construction zone.

Tom and the children were up and busy with secret preparations for Maggie's breakfast in bed, a Mother's Day treat. They had planned gourmet delights and tender attention. What they had was a mess in the kitchen. Or rather, the bedlam that passed for a kitchen.

The round oak table and chairs that had survived the tornado were all that remained in good condition. Tom had installed an old bathroom sink to use till the plumbers got to the kitchen. There were no cabinets and counter—just large baskets holding paper plates, towels, and odds and ends. A hot plate and a toaster stood on an ironing board that served as a makeshift counter. The kitchen was hardly the well-stocked room we had taken for granted before.

Baby Maura cooed and giggled in her infant seat on top of the table while Kathleen tried spooning a thin cereal mixture into the moving target that was her mouth. Because of the eight-year difference in their ages, Kathleen was part sister and part parent. I could see this was going to be a friendship to watch.

Three-year-old Annie Elizabeth was sitting on the table, too, close enough to kiss Maura's head now and then. Annie chuckled when the baby's downy blond hair tickled her nose.

Annie was pasting animal crackers on a shoe box, a very original Annie decoration-creation. I parked myself on the floor nearby, content to be in the middle of things.

It was a bad choice on my part.

An assortment of Magic Markers kept rolling off the table and smacking my head.

*Blonk. Blonk. Blonk.*

Annie scooted off the table, balanced herself on my back, and retrieved them. I might have minded, but she rewarded me with the same kind of gentle kiss she lavished on Maura.

*Smooch, pat. Smooch, pat. Smooch, pat.*

Annie and I were kindred spirits. She knew I was a sucker for affection.

Seth, the oldest, was at the hot plate stirring Cream of Wheat. The cereal was making the loud plopping noises of a boil, and little blobs were spitting onto the makeshift counter.

Tom, still in his pajamas and faded blue robe, came in the back door holding the season's first white rose from Maggie's favorite bush. When he closed the door, the plywood that passed for the east wall shook.

"We need a vase, Kathleen, or something to hold this flower." Tom was searching unsuccessfully through the supply baskets.

"Mom put a couple of boxes of kitchen stuff in the hall closet," Kathleen said. She knew the whereabouts of everything. I could picture a tiny computer behind her eyebrows filing and shuffling all that organizational genius.

"I found a chipped blue vase out by the apple trees when we first cleaned up after the tornado," Seth said. "I think I saw Mom pack it in that closet."

I felt a thud on my back as Annie bounded down. "I get it!"

I followed Annie's little red sneakers through the construction maze. It was like a

dainty ballet dancer leading a Russian tank, and I don't need to point out who represented what. By the time I reached the closet, Annie had unloaded a third of a box. She was playing soldier with a spatula and a wooden spoon. I figured the distraction would keep her busy for a while, so I looked for the vase myself. When I couldn't find it, I picked up the best substitute, the bottom half of an orange plastic thermos.

I carried it to the kitchen.

Kathleen took the thermos from my mouth. "This isn't exactly Waterford crystal!"

"It's got about as much class as the Cream of Wheat," Seth said. "I can't seem to keep the lumps out."

Seth was trying to mush a big one with a fork against the side of the pan.

"Put a little extra brown sugar on top and a cherry in the middle, and no one will notice," Kathleen suggested.

Seth did. "It looks like a volcano."

"Before or after?" Kathleen laughed.

"During." Seth sighed.

"It doesn't matter," Tom said. "If Maggie won't eat it, the Judge will."

I think I was being put down, but everyone was smiling, so I didn't take offense. Actually, the lumps were the best part, if you were lucky enough to find one in a crust of brown sugar.

"Did you butter the toast, Dad?" Kathleen was cleaning Maura's chin.

*"The toast!"*

One sniff told me what the smoking toaster told them.

Tom had found the toaster in the hedge after the tornado. Though it was free of dents and the coils heated, it had since refused to pop up. Trauma, I suppose, from the storm. Whatever, if someone didn't pop it up manually, it was Toast Crispies.

"Drat!" Tom held up the charred bread.

Seth was trying not to laugh. "Maybe we could scrape it."

Annie came back in with the only "vase" she could find in that hall closet box—a Tupperware cheese shredder.

Well, it *was* blue. She handed it to Tom.

"Oh, yukkk!" she said when she saw the toast.

"I'm with you, Annie. Let's not scrape it, let's scrap it," Tom decided.

"Judge might want it," Kathleen said.

Now, that was going too far. I raised the wrinkle over my eyes and turned up my nose. I had my pride.

Kathleen hugged my neck. "Oh, Judge, I didn't mean to insult you! Suppose I spread a little cream cheese on it?"

Cream cheese? I was weakening. If she would dot that with honey . . .

"Kathleen, no time for that. We better deliver this to Maggie before the Cream of Wheat gets cold. Just jelly some bread instead of waiting for more toast," Tom said.

Kathleen took three seconds to spread an

extra jelly bread. No one noticed when she slipped it to me.

Ah, homemade strawberry preserves!

"Seth, carry Maura," Tom directed. "I'll get the tray; Annie, you bring your box; and Kathleen, get the other presents."

I pranced in front of Tom, panting eagerly. Tom couldn't ignore me lest my enthusiasm sabotage the whole deal.

"O.K., Judge, you bring the paper."

It wasn't much, but it was a part, and I was up to it—even though it was an enormous Sunday edition. Heck, if somebody had asked me, I would have managed the unabridged dictionary.

My mouth could open *that wide*.

# Chapter 2

We made quite a parade winding down the cluttered hallway at 7:00 A.M. When Tom suggested a song, Annie Elizabeth chimed, "The Eentsy Weentsy Spider," but it came out more like "Easy Weasy Cider." Maggie was awakened by a cackling chorus.

"Oh, I love it! What a surprise!" Maggie was glowing.

Tom set up Maura's infant seat on the pillow by Maggie. Then we all presented our wares.

Breakfast wouldn't have passed for a ritzy catered job, but Maggie's oohs and aahs were sincere. Tom had squeezed fresh orange juice, though I never did see him locate the orange squeezer. I wondered what he had used—the Tupperware cheese shredder?

The jelly bread was a delightful change from toast, and the Cream of Wheat was scrumptious. Or so Maggie said. To prove it, she ate every single bite.

The cooks were appropriately charmed. I was only a little disappointed that Maggie hadn't shared her jelly bread with me.

"All these presents, for me?" Maggie had set aside the tray to make room for the boxes.

"Mine's the best." Annie Elizabeth climbed on the bed and thumped her bottom on Maggie's knee. Then Annie plunked her shoe box on Maggie's stomach.

"Oh, this is certainly special!" Maggie smiled.

Maggie caressed the shoe box lovingly. "I have just the place for it."

While Maggie was examining it, one of the animal crackers loosened and caught on the bedspread. If Annie had seen it fall, she would have cried. Her handiwork, ruined! Maggie slyly slipped the cracker to me for immediate disposal.

It was mildly yukky with all that paste, but I didn't mind. It was a small price for Annie's pride.

Kathleen's gift was a hand-knit potholder, large and bright yellow.

"Oh, beautiful!" Maggie exclaimed. "We lost most of the old ones in the tornado!"

Kathleen beamed. "We made it at Girl Scouts. I hope I got the color right for the new kitchen."

"It's perfect. In fact, when I order the new window shades, I'm going to bring this along and ask for 'potholder yellow'." Maggie gave Kathleen a hug, and soon Kathleen was sitting on the big bed beside Maggie's other knee.

"This isn't exactly a present," Seth began as he handed Maggie a piece of paper rolled up like a scroll and tied with a shiny red ribbon.

"'Course it is." Annie said. "See the bow."

Seth sat on the bed by Maggie. "What I mean, well, it's just a poem. I guess it's dumb, but . . ."

". . . but you spent your allowance on Milky Ways . . ." Kathleen put in.

". . . but I wanted to give you something no one else could . . ." Seth gave Kathleen his best big-brother glare, then smiled at Maggie.

Maggie's eyes were misting as she read the paper. "May I read it aloud?"

Seth nodded.

Maggie read:

> Other Mom's are good. But mine is dandy.
> No one else makes better Christmas candy.

Kathleen and Annie started to laugh, but Tom gave them a *shhhh* sign.

Maggie continued:

> Mom washes closes, she grosury shops,
> So what if her dives are belly flops.

Maggie winked at Seth.

> She works a lot and gives out hugs.
> And she's only afrade of great big bugs.
> We have fun, my mom and me her son.
> Yes she's the best
> in the north-east-south and west.

Maggie squeezed Seth's shoulder. "I'm thrilled, Seth. I'll frame this and keep it forever."

Seth kissed his mom on the cheek. Kathleen pretended to ignore him.

Tom pulled his present out from under the bed. It was a very large box. Maggie unwrapped a huge picnic basket. "Oh, it's perfect!" she exclaimed.

Indeed it was.

There were all the supplies you could think of attached with elastic bands: silverware and stem glasses for six, a bottle opener, a can opener, and serving spoons. There was a stack of plastic plates, a tablecloth and six matching red-checked napkins in several side pockets. Baskets in assorted sizes filled the bottom—one for bread, one with a tile bottom for cutting cheese, and one already holding jars of preserves and gourmet peanut butter. There was also a special thermal pocket in the back for ice and iced foods.

Wow. Tom's head was in the right place. My tummy could vouch for that.

Tom scooted up on the bed next to Seth and handed Maggie an envelope. "Happy Mother's Day, hon."

Maggie read it aloud, too.

WE, YOUR FAMILY, REQUEST THE HONOR OF YOUR PRESENCE AT A SPECIAL PICNIC DOWN THE LANE BY THE BIG DOUBLE OAK WHERE WE CAN TOAST YOU, FAMILY STYLE.

"I lovingly accept!"

"Will you eggscept me?" Annie wanted to know.

Kathleen giggled. "It's for the family, Annie. You're family."

I hoped that included me.

Tom added, "We've made something else, Maggie. You know that canvas sling you wore when you carried Annie as a baby?"

"Sure, I can dig that up."

"We already did," Tom said. "And we used it as a pattern for another one, a double sling— to fit a certain Saint Bernard." He winked in my direction. "It will help when you need to carry extra diapers for special outings." He handed Maggie the homemade carrier.

Like today, I hoped. I didn't want to be left guarding the house when a picnic was in the wind.

Tom must have read my mind. "Like today."

It was all so exciting. Everyone was clapping. I wanted to get a better look at that sling and the gourmet peanut butter.

I braced my paw against the side of the mattress and pulled myself up.

A cinch.

Then we heard a peculiar sound. It was a bit like a Roman candle going off on the Fourth of July.

Tom caught Annie, and Maggie grabbed Maura.

Kathleen and Seth rolled over on me, laughing.

I landed with a superthud, breaking everybody's fall.

When bed slats break, a Saint Bernard has to have grace under pressure. I was glad it was not a waterbed.

Even so, if it hadn't been Mother's Day, I might have been in real trouble.

But even Tom laughed. "You, Judge, have the paw that broke the mattress's back!"

Annie said, "The front's broke, too!"

Seth put the big yellow potholder on his head and sang out, "Save me! Save me! Dog underboard!"

There were no casualties. No bruises, no scrapes, nothing broken in the picnic basket, but, oh, my pride! That was wounded.

Baby Maura, instead of being frightened, added to the chorus of laughter with a full little gurgle in the back of her throat.

Still, I felt pretty foolish.

"Those slats should have been replaced long ago, Judge." Maggie was patting my shoulder. "Why, this bed is as old as all of us put together!"

Kathleen was resting on my other shoulder, still chuckling. She would be hiccupping soon.

Well, things could be worse. But maybe I'd pass up desserts for a couple of days.

"Now," Maggie went on, "what do we have to do to get ready for this picnic?"

That was the maternal signal for busy time.

# Chapter 3

"Seth, let's get started fixing this bed," Tom said.

"I'll finish packing the picnic basket," Kathleen volunteered.

"Annie, why don't you and the Judge keep me company while I bathe Maura." Maggie knew neither of us would miss that.

It didn't take a minute before we were all off and running. Annie and I took front-row center spots to watch Maura's bath.

Maura's delight was instant.

"Kin I hold her?" Annie was pushing the soap and making *putt putt* noises like a motorboat.

"No. Just watch and you'll know what to do when you're a mother."

"I'm going to be a daddy inztead. Was I dis small?"

"Mmmhmmm—but it was a long time ago." Maggie smiled away a chuckle. "Hand me that towel, honey."

Maggie dried Maura, then carried her to the

dressing table. Annie skipped at her heels, and I fell in line behind them.

My nose was exactly the right height to rest on the dressing table where I could see little Maura wiggling and cooing. There were treasures of soft-smelling things—the baby powder, the oil, the cotton balls, the freshly laundered clothes. Sometimes Maura's tiny foot would kick so hard, it got close enough to tickle my whiskers.

Annie climbed on the windowsill behind the table and made alphabet designs with the cotton swabs. "Her head is puffing," she said.

"Puffing? Oh, the soft spot!" Maggie held the baby with one hand and guided Annie's hand to the fleshy gap on top of Maura's head where her baby skull had not completed its growth. "Very gently, put your fingers here. All babies have this at first. As Maura gets older it will change, but now it's very delicate and you can feel her breathe. It's called the fontanel."

Annie thought about that. Then she stepped along the windowsill so that she was right by me. With both hands, Annie started parting the fur on my forehead. "I wanna see if the Judge has a fountain."

Maggie laughed. "No, Annie. He's as hardheaded as the rest of the O'Rileys."

I hoped that was a joke.

Annie didn't let go of my head. I was in place to be a convenient baby model. She experi-

mented with the cotton swabs, then reached for the baby powder.

I headed for the kitchen. I had my dignity to preserve.

Seth and Tom had finished fixing the bed and were helping Kathleen pack the food. The picnic basket was on the table. I couldn't see inside it, but my sense of smell gave me a pretty accurate accounting of the menu.

There was salami . . . good garlic-laced Genoa salami . . . some kind of cheese, probably Havarti since that was Maggie's favorite . . . cold turkey . . . bread. I could hear the crinkle of plastic bags, which probably meant potato chips and Fritos. There were oranges and bananas . . . and chocolate . . . chocolate something. Mercy! Brownies!! Talk about a tempting dessert.

Maybe if I skipped the potato chips . . .

Tom saw me take a place near the table. "Judge, for once your timing is perfect."

For once?

Seth got the sling off the back of a chair. "Hope this fits, Judge."

It did.

The strappings were made of a stretchy fabric with adjustable cinches so a load could be either large or small. A piece of foam lined the wide cross at the shoulders, for comfort. The canvas zippered pockets were dark tan, and someone (my sixth sense voted for Kathleen) had ironed patches on them—pictures of famous dogs—Lassie, Kavik, Little Benji, and Buck.

My sense of worth was returning. After the bed fiasco, it felt good to be in the company of the classics.

Annie came running in just then. "Oh, goodee! I'm gonna pack the Judge!"

I could picture Annie trying to fold me into a piece of Samsonite luggage.

"O.K., Annie. Put some diapers in and a lightweight blanket," said Tom.

Annie also added two stuffed bunnies and a one-eared teddy bear. She was trying to include a Fisher-Price castle when Kathleen stopped her.

"Annie! We can't take the kitchen sink, you know!"

"'Course not. It's stuck on the wall," Annie answered.

Seth took the castle from Annie and handed her a small red top. "Here, Annie. Let's pack this instead. It's Maura's favorite."

Annie was persuaded.

Maggie came out carrying Maura in her sling. Both were dressed for the hike. Maggie put a box of diaper wipers and a couple of trash bags in my pack.

"My, it looks like you have everything under control." Maggie smiled approvingly.

"Just say the word and we go," Tom said.

"O.K."—Maggie snapped her fingers—"Go!"

We did, though there was a brief moment of confusion when Tom, carrying the picnic basket, and a certain Saint Bernard, wearing saddlebags, tried to exit through the front door at the same time.

Once outside, I led the way.

The picnic spot was just over the big hill, and I was eager to get there. It was a favorite spot—the old oak kept the ground around it cool and shady and held the tire swing that each O'Riley child had loved. I looked back at Tom for permission to take off running.

"Sure, sport, go ahead," he said when he saw my expression. "Just don't drop your parcels."

I ran over the hill at a good gallop in spite of my new saddlebags.

I was the first to see it.

# Chapter 4

It looked like a great gleaming white bus, twenty-seven feet long with a broad band of tinted glass across the front and on the sides. The name on the shiny aluminum was PACE ARROW.

It was so big I could look the headlights right in the eye. The tire tops were level with my withers. I walked around it, searching for signs of life.

But I couldn't find anyone. Not in the Pace Arrow, not at the picnic table, not by the creek behind the big oak.

What was it doing at our spot on this very special day?

When Tom walked up with the family, he gave me my answer. He pressed a set of keys in Maggie's hand.

"You're looking at our new motor home."

Maggie was stunned.

Tom kept talking. "And you once said I couldn't keep a secret. Well, this time the whole family gets to enjoy your Mother's Day surprise. We can live in it now, while construction peaks on the interior of the house. And later . . ."

When it finally soaked in, it was an O'Riley circus.

The children didn't wait to hear about later. The chorus of squeals drowned out any trivial conversation. There was a minor stampede to get in and check *it* out.

Maggie unlocked the main door and Kathleen vaulted in. "Wait, Kathleen! I haven't got the entry step out," yelled Tom, struggling unsuccessfully to pull it down. Seth couldn't wait and hoisted Annie over Tom's shoulders. Then Seth lifted himself in. Maggie was still standing outside the camper, giving advice to Tom on releasing the step, so I couldn't see much.

But I could hear the children's delight.

"A microwave! Seth, look!"

"Swivel chairs! This one's mine."

"Two couches . . . and look at all these drawers."

"Oh, goodee! A potty."

"Hey, this couch opens up."

"And it has blue water. Boy, it makes a funny sound when you flush it."

"Annie, don't play with that."

The step still wouldn't budge, and Maggie was getting impatient. "Tom, I can't wait. Forget the step."

Tom boosted Maggie up and stepped in, too. Maura just missed bumping her head since the backpack made her taller than Maggie, but then she was inside, too. I almost got a paw in the door, but the screen door slammed behind Tom.

No one seemed to notice.

"This is really something! I love these earthy colors."

"And it has a retractable awning and storage on top. Just wait until you drive it."

"Oh, may I?"

"Sure, what's wrong with now?"

"Well, Maura . . ."

"Here, I'll take her."

There must have been a tape deck, because from somewhere I heard a loud spunky version of "Another One Bites the Dust." Then I heard the ignition and the motor.

I barked, but they didn't hear me.

The music was blaring.

That fast, they left without me.

It was pretty clear who was biting the dust. For the first time all day, my load began to feel heavy. I sat down to shift it.

They'd be back of course. After all, I had Maura's diapers.

As I watched the shiny new motor home fade out of sight, I felt lonely as heck. I had this peculiar knotting in my stomach.

There was nothing to do but wait—until they remembered their old Saint Bernard, or needed a diaper, whichever came first.

And then I noticed the picnic basket.

They'd left in such a hurry that it was still

sitting at the side of the road where Tom first put it down.

Hmmmmmmmmmmmmmmmmm.

I got this picture in my mind of a warm chocolate brownie, the powdered sugar melting on top . . .

The camper was nowhere in sight.

Would they miss just one?

The picnic basket had a simple latch closure, one peg inside one loop. A pussycat could have handled it.

I knew better, but that had never stopped me before. I had worked up quite an appetite hauling my pack, and it might be hours before they returned.

My tongue pushed the peg through the loop, and my big nose easily flipped the lid.

I really meant to have just one brownie . . . but they weren't on top the way I thought they'd be. And I had this slight handicap. While I was trying to maneuver my nose and paw to move things around, the zipper on my saddlebags got caught on the can opener attached to the lid. When I twisted my body to free myself, I lost my balance.

My right paw landed on a wheel of soft Havarti cheese. I could feel an oozing sensation slither all the way up to my dewclaw.

Yukk.

It was an irreversible goof.

There was no turning back. I decided to eat my way to the brownies.

# Chapter 5

I'll never forget the "Shame on you" faces that came out of the shiny new camper. There I stood, a can opener on the zipper of the sling, a hunk of wax paper in my collar, and breathing garlic like a dragon breathing fire.

I couldn't expect high marks for good behavior.

I was roundly scolded.

They stripped me of my sling.

Tom, irritated and disappointed, simply raised his arm and pointed his finger toward home.

As they drove off in search of Kentucky Fried Chicken to replace the picnic I'd eaten, I walked back to the house.

A nap on the front porch brought no relief, only nightmares of a lonely Saint banished to an island with apple trees and no children.

When they came home hours later, I couldn't look at the camper without pangs of guilt.

They parked it at the end of the driveway, and Tom set out the gloriously cheerful gold-striped awning. Seth dragged lawn chairs and Maura's red wind-up-swing from the garage. Kathleen propped Maura up with pillows, and Maggie turned the crank of the automatic swinging device as far as it could go.

I decided after my booboo that it was better to be unseen and unheard, so I slipped to a spot by the birch tree and listened.

"I luf it so much," Annie was saying.

"Can we move our stuff in tonight?" Kathleen asked.

"I get the bunk. Remember, you promised, I get the bunk," Seth said.

"No and yes," Maggie answered, "in that order. I think we need a day to pare down our wants and whims before we go overstocking and have no room for passengers."

"Right, kids," Tom agreed. "Compared with the big house, this is a very little home. Tomorrow we'll assign cubbyholes and limit what we need to the bare essentials. We only have to make do for a little while—till the remodeling is done."

"You mean it's just that—a temporary house?" Seth asked.

"Funny you asked," Tom said, smiling. "As a matter of fact, as long as we have it, I thought in two weeks, when school is out, we might just take off for parts unknown!"

Parts unknown?

I scooted to a spot by Tom's chair so I could hear plainly.

"Great!" Seth was jumping up and down. "We'll be roughing it, right?"

I heard Maggie groan.

"Roughing it?" Kathleen commented. "With hot and cold water and a microwave?"

"I was referring to the bugs and bears in the wilderness," Seth replied.

"Well, I guess you could call some of Canada the wilderness," Tom said.

Canada?

"Dad, what bugs and bears?" asked Kathleen.

"Iiillck. I'll take the bears over the bugs," Maggie said.

"Can I play wid the baby bears?" It was Annie's turn to talk.

"Best you bring your Paddington Bear and forget about the live ones. There will be no playing with bears, and there will be no catching bugs to scare sisters and mothers." Maggie looked sternly at Seth.

Seth didn't say anything but he hid a grin.

But Canada?

It occurred to me that as big as the camper was, I was a bit big for it, and the plans just could mean . . .

"How many miles?"

"How long will we be gone?"

"Three *whole* weeks?"

"Is Canaday more'n free blocks away?"

"Where will Judge Benjamin ride?"

I heard the questions mount, the reality hitting me like a coconut cream pie with a rock hidden in its crust. Tom answered them all—except the last question.

The pause made me sick to my stomach.

Then, quite calmly, he said, "We're going to need someone around home to keep an eye on the remodeling. Thank goodness we have the Judge." He patted my head, and it reminded me of someone plugging in the electric chair.

The quiet was incredible.

Even Maggie looked stunned.

Finally, Annie whimpered, "No Judge Benjamin? For free weeks?"

Tom spoke again. He was looking at Maggie. "It's the only practical thing. Mr. Lockley can feed him while we're away, and it will be a good idea to have him around nights with the house under construction."

Maggie still didn't say anything.

Tom kept up his argument. "After all, where would we *put* a Saint Bernard? Really, Maggie!!!"

Seth and Kathleen said nothing.

Tom was clearly disappointed. Instead of the happy planning of a few minutes before, he was facing a crowd of mourners. "Look," he said, "this is a rare opportunity for any family, and the Judge is a fine animal and he'll understand."

Animal? As in lion and tiger and chipmunk? Who's he kidding?

"He would want us to go and have a wonderful time." Tom gave me another pat on the head.

No, I wouldn't. No, I didn't. Selfish or not, I didn't like the idea at all.

Maura started to fuss, and Maggie picked her up and paced with her.

Annie's whimper turned into an honest-to-goodness cry. She came over to wipe her tears on my neck.

"O.K.," Tom said sternly. "Everybody to bed. The decision's made. We'll move into the camper tomorrow, and in two weeks we'll take off for Canada without Judge, and we'll all have a good time whether you like it or not!!"

# Chapter 6

No one went to bed smiling, least of all me.

I watched the lights go out in the big house and tried to make myself comfortable enough to catch a few winks.

The warm, clear day had turned into a muggy night. Summer was close, very close, and it would be a typically humid Decatur June, for sure. Of course, in Canada, it would be cool and pleasant.

I swallowed hard to get the lump out of my throat.

Three weeks without little Maura pulling the hair on my ears . . . without Annie Elizabeth putting electric rollers in my tail . . . without Seth and Kathleen playing keepaway . . .

And suppose there were bears in Canada? Who would warn my family? Or if they got lost, who would find them? I would be miles away, guarding a bunch of bricks and wood. If there was a way for me to join the traveling party, I intended to find it.

I needed to get a good look inside the camper.

After school the next day, when the packing began in earnest, I finally got to see things for myself.

Tom took Maggie, Annie, and Kathleen into town to get some supplies for the trip and left Seth and me behind to baby-sit Maura.

Seth set Maura up in her playpen under the crab apple tree and then turned to me. "Wanna see the camper, Judge? Inside?"

Are you kidding? This was the chance I had been waiting for!

I wagged my tail in unbounded gratitude.

The camper that loomed so enormously in the driveway appeared much less roomy from an inside view. It was nice, quite nice, built to handle everything *except* Saint Bernard traffic.

Seth grabbed the bottle of dishwashing detergent from on top of the sink and waved it in front of his mouth like a microphone. "Note, first, the sleeping accommodations . . ."

Accommodations? Funny, I'd never heard him use that big word before. But he evidently knew what it meant.

"These two couches on either side, but not directly opposite, form double beds," Seth said with a sweep of his hand. After a brief pause to lay down his "microphone" and pull one couch into sleeping position, he went on. "This bunk"—he waved in the direction above the driver's seat—"suits a single nicely." A single? I could tell by his smile that he had chosen the "single accommodation" for himself.

Seth sat in the cushy driver's seat and swiveled to face me. He pointed and gestured dramatically, "The custom kitchen . . ."

By the time he had itemized everything, from the small bathroom with tub and shower in the back to the tape deck and tables in the front, I was convinced of one thing.

It was quite a package deal. It could oblige just about every need.

Except one. Me.

I never thought I'd wish to be a chihuahua.

During Seth's tour, I was quite the captive audience. I first went forward, then backed the length of the camper, because, with the tables in place and couch pulled down, a Saint Bernard simply could not turn around.

When Maura began to fuss and Seth left to tend her, I stayed behind and studied the situation.

I got on the front couch and lay down to do some mental arithmetic. When I stood up, I had plenty of head room and could see out those great big windows. But how was I going to get around?

Maybe the secret was to walk on everything above the floor.

By golly, what could happen?

I stood on the couch and turned west. From the couch to the coffee table was simple enough. Front paws on table, back paws on couch. Then right front paw to swivel chair, back right paw to coffee table . . . one . . . two

. . . left front paw, same, left back paw, same. . . . Great!

I guess I started to get a little cocky here. I forgot the key word in *swivel chair*.

Swivel.

When the two back paws left the coffee table to join their partners on the swivel chair, it swung around.

I tried to stop its swing by putting my paw on the window behind it.

The window didn't break, but my claws made their mark with a rip on the hem of the drape.

Darn.

Well, it was just a little rip. Maybe no one would notice.

I twirled till the chair stopped. Comfy chair, even for my two hundred pounds. But the rust color clashed with the auburn in my coat. It was time to move on.

I made it to the next couch easily, but I was followed by the window shade from the main door. It must have caught on my collar. I shook it free.

The next step tested my pioneer spirit to its limits—the bathroom. It had a potty befitting a terrier derrière. Thank goodness the lid was down.

I had to practically turn a corner in the jump, but Barnum and Bailey should have been watching. My two hundred pounds balanced perfectly on the toilet lid.

I admit I probably looked a bit peculiar, but it was the best seat in the house from which to study the camper lengthwise.

The tub was small, very small. If I got in that bit of Formica, I wasn't sure I could wiggle out.

The big closet across from the tub was airless. If I had thoughts of stowing away, I'd never make two miles in that.

The kitchen was all that was left. The counter was a toughie to plant my big paws on. I did fine but managed to turn on the exhaust fan over the stove as my ears sailed by.

Shelves were everywhere, but even a tall box of cereal was going to be a squeeze. There didn't seem to be anyplace for a Saint Bernard to sneak aboard.

But there was that bunk Seth showed me over the driver's seat . . .

If there were some way to flatten myself on that bunk without snapping it all the way down—or maybe in the storage behind it . . .

I overshot the bunk. My front side held, but my bottom side slid toward the dashboard. When I tried to scramble back onto the bunk, the bed sprung halfway back up, locking me into the most incredible position just above the driver's seat.

There I hung, shoulders above, my hips—not exactly made for Calvin Klein designer jeans—below, back paws dangling in the direction of the dash.

What happened next was a high point in personal humiliation.

Those paws picked the worst possible spot to land.

The horn.

It was the first time I had heard the horn, and at close range, it was worse than an air raid siren.

I kept shifting my paws, trying to land on something else, but all I managed to do was honk in staccato.

Seth came running up at the same time Maggie, Tom, Annie, and Kathleen pulled into the drive.

Maggie would say later that she thought the windshield wipers had been fur-equipped for weather, the way my tail was wagging in that great tinted window. But when reality hit her, all she could do was shriek.

From my peculiar perch, I suddenly became aware of my many goofs—the torn curtain, the broken shade, the switched-on fan, which had begun to blow the paper towels over the sink into a bizarre kind of sail . . .

As Annie would say, I was prolly in big tubble.

# Chapter 7

I guess I suspected right then and there that the camper welcome mat wouldn't be out for me—ever. Tom's vacation plans without a Saint Bernard made some sense to all the O'Rileys. Maggie and the kids weren't exactly doing handstands at the thought of my missing the trip, but they had become quietly resigned to Tom's decision.

I couldn't blame them. I knew I didn't deserve a reprieve.

The humid weather I had expected in late May never came. It was clear and bright and positively dry. I was able to sleep under the camper's awning all fourteen nights during my brief stay of execution. I gradually came to think of the awning post as *my* spot.

So did Annie.

She kept lining up things that she thought were canine furnishings—my old rug, my water bowl, a rubber newspaper.

I guessed Annie wasn't quite as resigned to my not going as everybody else. She didn't realize I would need a miracle to be included.

Departure was just a day away when Maggie got the bright idea to bless the camper.

"Bless what?" Tom couldn't believe it.

For that matter, neither could I.

"Bless the camper. It's our home, even if it is on wheels," Maggie said.

"Bless a motor home?" Tom was still confused.

"See, there are actually two blessings that could work—the one for a voyage and the one for a house." Maggie barely took a breath making her explanation.

"I can call the rectory, Mom. I know Father Leo would do it," Kathleen volunteered.

"No need, hon, I already have," Maggie said.

Tom shook his head, but he was smiling.

"And Sister Hermengilda is in town to take a parish census, so I invited her, too." Maggie just kept rambling. "And the Lockleys are so close, I thought they might like to stop by, and we could have kind of a sendoff dinner."

"Wow, a party!" Annie was clapping. "Kin we have balloons?"

Tom was laughing now. "Do I have to show up any special time, or am I included at all?"

The only one not smiling and enjoying the plans was Seth. "Sister Hermengilda? *The* Sister Hermengilda?" His face had gone white.

My heart beat a little faster. Sister Hermengilda? I had never heard of her, but there was something about that name . . .

"The choir leader? The eighth-grade English

teacher who puts fear in the hearts of thirteen-year-olds wishing to graduate in one piece?" Seth's voice was a bit shaky.

"Seth, she hasn't taught here in several years—and you and Kathleen have never had her. All the Dominican Sisters are just lovely." Maggie wasn't convincing Seth of anything.

"Mom, you just don't *know!* Some things are *legend!*" Seth was still white. "Why, I heard—"

Tom interrupted. "This will be a perfect opportunity to prove that what you hear isn't always to be believed. Prejudging is a very bad habit."

Seth didn't say any more, but he had certainly made me wonder. So the party was set.

The day was a busy one—last-minute packing, Maggie baking, trying to keep Annie out from underfoot. Tom had rigged an ingenious hoist to the storage space at the top of the camper. I sat beneath the roof ladder, watching the packing process. Annie made the most of the opportunity and polished my claws.

Even my back paws glimmered with Positively Peach Punch nail polish.

The hoist was a thick elastic strap, with a hook at the end, that was attached to a pulley on the camper roof. After an object was secured at the bottom—the heavier things were double-wound with the strap—someone on the roof of the camper cranked the pulley and the object made its way to the top. Seth worked the crank, and Tom stored the gear. Annie and

I watched as lawn chairs, suitcases, and even bikes were lifted into place. When Tom got a phone call in the big house, Seth switched jobs with Tom and Kathleen turned the crank. Maggie fastened things on the hook and strap from the ground. After Maggie fastened the last item, a Weber grill, in place, she too went into the house, leaving Seth and Kathleen to put away the hoist.

That's when Annie got her bright idea. She had been watching the whole procedure and had gotten it down pat. I heard her yell to Kathleen and Seth.

"One more ting, guys."

She grabbed the hook at the end of the hoist, and I knew.

Annie, no.

But she already had me roped and fastened.

I was sure the strap would break or the pulley would snap.

In spite of my two hundred pounds, I felt my paws kicking air.

I was two feet off the ground before Seth looked over the side of the camper to see what was coming.

Kathleen just cranked away. She would never in a million years have admitted that turning the load was a struggle.

"Kathleen!" Seth screamed. "Stop!"

"I can handle it, Seth," she said.

So there I dangled, Annie giggling, Seth in shock, Kathleen never pausing, when I saw a strange white figure whisking down our road.

The blessing and party were not scheduled for two more hours, but there, in all her glory, was *the* Sister Hermengilda.

She was riding her bike. Great waves of a white veil flapped behind her. Her long skirt was secured like bloomers with rubber bands. She wore her guitar on her back, and I heard her singing as she pulled into the drive.

Probably people for five miles heard her singing. Her soprano was *very* loud.

And that's when Kathleen finally looked up and let go.

With no one holding the crank . . .

what goes up . . .

must come down.

Ouch.

Sister Hermengilda was treated to anything but a five-gold-star first impression.

Kathleen climbed down the camper and unhooked me.

Seth stayed on top of the camper and hid behind the Weber grill.

"Good afternoon, Sister. We weren't expecting you quite so early," Kathleen said.

Nothing like the direct approach.

Sister Hermengilda got off her bike and stared at me.

She continued to stare as she pulled a Mickey Mouse pocket watch with a San Diego, California, streamer out of her habit.

Seth and Kathleen looked at each other and sighed. Now they had met the legend, complete with jet lag, and still operating on California time. Just our luck.

Seth climbed down the ladder.

I decided to try to erase the bad start with a fresh and formal introduction. I extended my paw . . .

. . . and made my second impression. A very dirty one. On her clean white habit. Well, at least my nail polish was dry. But I could see Sister's pupils widen behind those rimless glasses.

When she opened her mouth, it was not to say hello. It was to scream, the longest, shrillest soprano scream I had ever heard. The look in her eyes was—terror.

For a moment I understood what it must have felt like to flunk eighth-grade English.

When Seth unstrapped me, I escaped to the security of out-of-sight, out-of-mind, and hid behind the garbage cans.

It was a long two hours for Seth and Kathleen to entertain Sister Hermengilda before everyone else arrived. Besides the guitar, Sister had two different pitch pipes, and she wasn't satisfied until the whole family—even Tom—joined her minichoir. I had never realized there were so many verses in "Amazing Grace."

Father Leo was the last guest to arrive. He brought along his dad, who was visiting him in town, a slight man who captured Annie's immediate fancy with his Yo-Yo tricks. He brought his own Yo-Yo, a silver and blue Duncan classic. Father Leo's mom had sent a big box of homemade jellies and jams for Maggie to take on the trip.

The camper was loaded to the gills, but Maggie wouldn't have refused the gesture for anything. She sent Seth and Kathleen to hoist it up to the storage area.

I was a little nervous about what my two hundred pounds might have done to the hoist, so I moved in for a better look. Even elastic can't stretch forever.

Sister Hermengilda took charge of herding everyone else to the picnic table in front of the camper for the blessing ceremony. Father Leo, holding the candle and holy water Sister had planted in his hands, took a few minutes to walk around the camper.

His timing couldn't have been worse.

As the case of jellies eased their way up the side of the camper, the strap began to pull apart.

I barked to warn him, but all he did was freeze.

I had no choice. I came running, hoping to push him out of the way.

Sister Hermengilda, whose spine had no doubt tingled at the sound of my bark, came dashing around the camper to issue her own warning about Saint Bernards that fly.

I lunged and knocked Father Leo to his knees. He thought I was attacking and started sprinkling holy water all over me. "Peace be to you, Saint Bernard . . ." He was trembling.

That's gratitude. And with my kind face, yet.

When the hoist finally snapped, Father Leo was out of its way. But Sister Hermengilda, first shrieking, then blessing herself, then shrieking some more, had dashed at full speed directly into the path of a jar of blackberry jam that had escaped the case.

It painted her habit with color.

Well, anyway, it was an interesting blue, and it hid the spot my paw had made earlier.

# Chapter 8

At least on the last night I went to bed a hero.

Maggie and Tom calmly explained my honorable intentions to Sister and Father. The Lockleys and other neighbors were character witnesses citing past examples of my virtue, until finally everyone laughed and at least agreed that my motives had been sincere. Father Leo and Sister Hermengilda even chanted new verses of "Bless the Beasts and the Children" that included my name in the same phrase with thanks.

Sister Hermengilda patted me on the head when she said good-bye—though she did ask to wash her hands right afterward.

Maggie decided that the family would sleep in the big house instead of the camper. She wanted to start the trip with clean sheets.

Because the kids' rooms were being worked on, they put sleeping bags in the dining room for the final night in the big house. Maura slept in her car bed by the dry sink. I curled up in the corner by the corn plant with Annie next to me.

I couldn't sleep at all. Knowing they'd be on the road without me for several weeks made me feel peculiar. Would they be all right? Would they miss me?

Seth and Kathleen were so excited that they closed their eyes immediately. The packing and the party must have worn them out. Or maybe they just thought it could make the morning come quickly. But Annie—Annie kept tossing and turning.

Suddenly, she sat straight up and whispered, "Judge? I thing they all wan you to come. Big guys are silly sometimes, but we'll fix it."

She began tugging at my collar. "I luf you, Judge. Shhh, now, let's go. Pease?"

I couldn't imagine what she had in mind.

"C'mon, Judge, this is our big shance!"

Then she kissed me.

That did it.

I would have followed her to Alaska. But all she wanted was for me to follow her to the Pace Arrow. Foolish, I thought. There could be no hiding me, if that's what she had in mind. You don't slide a Saint Bernard between two bookends and hope he'll pass unnoticed. They'd find me, scold me, and abandon me as planned, but for a few hours, Annie would be satisfied.

So I went.

The step wasn't pulled out. I made a body

bridge, and Annie scooted up my back and slid down my neck onto the rust-colored carpet.

I could tell from her *Wheee!* that there was a new game in town.

The camper looked even smaller than I'd remembered, probably because of all the supplies.

"Now," Annie wondered out loud, "where you go?"

It was a good question.

There wasn't a good answer.

I would have given up right then. But not Annie.

"O.K., Judge, into the bathtub!"

The bathtub? The only spot in the camper that I hadn't trusted myself to explore the last time? That little square patch of Formica? It would take a tow truck to get the likes of me out of it!

Annie was clapping. "It will be perfeck! The gurtain can hide you."

That little thing? Like putting a shower cap on a mountain lion? Like expecting a hairnet to hold back Niagara Falls? Annie!

". . . and you like the tub in the big house . . ."

I wanted to remind Annie that the tub in the big house was a large steeping bath that would have held two Saint Bernards nicely, but . . .

She was pushing my bottom with all her might when I looked up and saw a strange reflection in the medicine cabinet mirror—a

narrow strip of light. We were about to be discovered!

"Annie! What are you up to?"

Seth appeared, waving his flashlight.

I thought Annie might cry, but she faced him squarely, those little hands stuck on her hips. Her voice punched the air with authority. "Judge is comin' and I'm hidin' him and you bedder not tell, or I'll . . . I'll . . ."

I don't know what threat she might have come up with, but Seth was at her side, smiling, not scolding.

"Annie, this is just crazy!" He studied the strange scene for a minute, Annie's determined face, my front paws in the little tub. "What the heck. If you want to try, we will. Here, I'll give Judge a boost."

My nose hit the Formica first, followed by two hundred pounds. The squash was incredible. If my nose had been an accordion, it would have been playing a polka as I squished and squeezed to redistribute my weight from my nose to a more reasonable posture.

Seth tried to help, but it was one of those mathematical equations where so many square inches could only fit so many square pounds one way.

My tail kept popping out the side.

Annie kept tucking it in.

Pop.

Tug.

Seth finally took the strip of plastic that tied the shower curtain to the wall and bound my tail to my back leg. Then he pulled the curtain across my body.

He peeked around the side.

"Well, Judge, you're in. If you can stand it, it just might work."

Standing would have been wonderful. My muscles were squeezed to aching, but I was willing to risk it.

And then we heard another voice.

"What's going on here?"

It was Kathleen.

She didn't wait for an answer; she came in and saw for herself.

"I don't believe this. You're all crazy," she said, frowning at Seth.

"Aw, c'mon, Kathleen." Seth was winking at her and nodding toward Annie. "We have to try it for Annie's sake."

Kathleen pulled on her collar and bit her lower lip.

"Well, if we're going to do this, we better do it right," she said finally. "What about Gaines-burgers? And how about his leash?"

She was ticking off details, and soon they were scrambling back into the house to take care of them.

"Don't wake Maura, whatever you do!" Seth turned off the flashlight and led the way in darkness.

I wondered if we weren't forgetting something. Didn't I need some kind of papers to leave the country? Maggie had packed birth certificates for everyone else. . . . But in my present state, I was so folded, spindled, and mutilated, all I could think of was surviving the night.

I remembered hearing a story about the Trojan horse—how men hid inside a large wooden replica of a horse and conquered a town—and I wondered if history would record a camper hiding a huge Saint Bernard who just wanted to conquer a simple family vacation.

Amid my fantasies of fame, I finally fell asleep.

# Chapter 9

Pain was the order of the dawn.

Pain in my joints, pain in my claws, pain in my earlobes. Every muscle had fallen into a tingly sleep or rebelled in an ache.

There hadn't been much choice. I couldn't back out of Annie's plan now.

I heard the commotion in the big house that always went with last-minute preparations.

I knew it was just a matter of time before I was discovered and had to say good-bye.

The good news was that they had finished packing the camper before I'd been assigned my hiding place.

The bad news was that I'd forgotten the visibility problem Tom had when backing the camper out of the driveway. Someone had to go to the rear of the van—which was the bathroom and my hiding spot—and call out directions by looking out the far back window. It was a safety measure Tom insisted on because of the blind spot in rear-view mirrors.

It meant, if the someone was Maggie, that I

probably wouldn't even get out of the driveway before I was bounced.

Annie was the first one in the camper, holding her favorite faded unicorn and Paddington Bear in one hand and a lunchbox in another. I could see her from a little corner where the shower curtain was folded back. She glanced in my direction and put a *shhh* finger to her lips.

Annie, dear, whom would I tell?

Kathleen and Seth were right behind her, both with pillows and both glancing sideways to see how I'd survived the night.

Maggie came in carrying Maura, and Tom followed with Maura's car bed. They wedged it firmly into a spot at the end of the kitchen counter and by the couch so it wouldn't slide and then rigged a safety strap over the top.

Maura's eyes were open wide. She seemed to be enjoying the adventure already.

"Are you sure we have everything?" Tom asked.

"I'm not sure at all," Maggie answered, laughing. "But I'm not checking even once more! Let's go, please!"

Tom got out of the camper one more time to talk to the construction men who had just driven up. He was giving explicit instructions about completing the job by the time we returned. Mr. Lockley stopped by, too, and there was another delay while Tom repeated the same instructions and handed him some keys.

"Oh, and about the Judge . . ." Tom began.

Uh-oh.

"Where is he?"

Seth was out of the camper in a flash. "Oh, I put him out back, and he went for a walk. He hates good-byes."

Mr. Lockley actually believed him.

Seth's face was crimson. I couldn't remember the last time he fibbed. A vision of Sister Hermengilda appeared in my head, and I was overwhelmed with guilt.

While they were talking, Maggie got up to get a toy for Maura from the cabinet under the sink.

Like lightning, Kathleen intercepted her.

"Whatcha need, Mom? I'll get it."

Maggie was puzzled but asked for the music ball. When the cabinet door was opened, I could see a large box of Gainesburgers and my leash. Kathleen hid them with her body and handed Maggie the ball.

Finally, Tom came back in. He got in the driver's seat and told Maggie to go to the back.

This is it, I thought.

Seth and Kathleen shouted at once, "I'll direct!"

Maggie looked at them, confused. It was the first time the two had volunteered together, ever.

"No," Maggie said firmly. "We'll not begin this trip with you two fighting for favors."

Seth and Kathleen looked at each other. In their haste to fool Maggie, they'd blown it.

I tried to squeeze my two hundred pounds

into oblivion behind the shower curtain. Maybe she wouldn't notice.

Maggie was less than a foot away.

Please don't look this way, I thought.

But in that instant, our eyes met. Some instinct, some something had caused her to look toward the tub. There, overflowing the rim, was a coat of tan and auburn fur, a black nose that made a dark shadow against the plastic shower curtain, and one eye peeking through a fold in the flimsy material.

I sighed. It was over.

But a funny thing happened.

Maggie didn't say a word. She just began to smile. A big friendly smile followed by a wink. Then, just as the big camper was about to move, the smile vanished.

"Tom!" she shouted. "I forgot to unplug the iron!"

Iron? Unplug the iron? Maggie hadn't used an iron since wash 'n' wear came on the scene. Unplug it?

Evidently Tom wasn't aware of that because he took it in stride. Patiently, he studied the map.

Maggie ran into the house and was out in minutes. In the pocket of her sweater, I could see a business-size paper that hadn't been there before. The letter heading was LARRY BAKER, D.V.M. My vet. So official papers *were* needed to get me out of the country.

The conspiracy was complete.

Instead of aches, I felt a peculiar numbness—gratitude, no doubt.

Maggie was talking from the back to Tom. "A little to the right . . . that's it . . . well, we're on our way, kids!"

This time she winked five times—to me . . . to Annie . . . to Seth . . . to Kathleen . . . even to Maura.

And the winks were answered with five very big smiles.

# Chapter 10

The camper rolled on and Decatur faded into the distance.

I truly ached, but I was still in heaven. Maybe Father Leo's holy water had inspired a miracle. This time, the family had not left without me. I wondered what marvelous adventures we could have in this strange traveling house.

The fear of discovery by Tom faded with the miles.

But then another small problem developed.

It had been roughly nine hours since I had been assigned my dubious post in the bathtub. Nature was beckoning. I really needed to find a fireplug or an obliging tree.

All the family—except Tom, of course—winked, smiled, and giggled in my direction at regular intervals. But when I responded to their affectionate recognition with grimaces of pain, no one seemed to understand my dilemma.

My need increased. When Annie, in her well-meaning way, presented me with a butter dish of water while Tom was distracted by traffic, it was the last straw.

I knew I had to get out.

I raised my body on the strength of my front legs, but it was a struggle. Worse, when I decided to enlist my back legs, there was the small matter of the shower curtain tie that attached my tail to my left leg.

No one noticed my struggle. Seth and Kathleen were both reading, Annie was singing to little Maura, and Maggie had dozed off on the back couch.

Since Maggie had gone to sleep, Tom, not wanting to awaken her, had assumed the role of navigator as well as driver.

He was lousy at it.

While I was struggling for balance in the back of the camper, Tom was trying to fold the map, hold the wheel, and keep his eyes on the road, all at the same time.

The combination was deadly.

He swerved and I swerved.

We swerved.

The next thing I knew, I was lost in a shroud of plastic shower curtain, and he was wiggling four tons of motor home down Interstate 72 North.

My body decided to go north also.

I didn't see what happened next; I only felt it.

The shower curtain was released from its snap closures on the curtain rod, and I was released with it.

The queer weight shift upset the balance within the motor home. A puzzled Tom looked in the rear-view mirror and watched a ball of me fling like a slingshot down the middle of the camper.

We wound up off the road just past a rest area, Tom screaming, "*Judge!* Is this a bad dream?" and me landing ungracefully at the foot of the CB radio.

Well, it did get everyone's attention.

While Tom faced the family conspirators, I decided not to witness the weeping and gnashing of teeth.

I struggled free of the shower curtain, lifted the handle on the door with a push of my nose . . . and found a tree.

# Chapter 11

We had come seventy-five miles into the trip, and Maggie and the kids were winning their case.

I was waiting outside the screen door, listening and hoping.

Tom tried to protest, but no one listened.

"We've come too far," Maggie said.

"We packed the Judge's things," Kathleen said.

"We'll make room," Seth said.

"I luf Judge and I'm not leabing wifout him."

After Tom had heard all the arguments, he remained silent. Then he got out of the camper and stood thoughtfully.

When he saw me, he patted my head and winked.

Now, what did that mean?

He climbed back inside and faced the family. "O.K., but he's on probation."

Everyone cheered. Especially when the door was opened and I was settled into a relaxing spot by the back couch.

Maggie and Seth fixed the shower curtain, and we were ready to roll.

The miles flew. I could barely believe my good fortune.

When Seth, Kathleen, and Annie started a game of cards on the floor, they let me have the big couch up front. I could see the whole world out those windows, and I loved it. Trees, lakes, traffic, people . . . and then . . . I saw her.

Tom had slowed the camper a bit as he tried to spot the turnoff to our first overnight campsite. A yellow station wagon pulling a Kit camper passed in the next lane. In the bed of the wagon was the most beautiful Irish setter I had ever laid eyes on.

Her molded head and long, clean neck fit smoothly into sloping shoulders. Her ears were low-set, the sure mark of a pedigree. Her dark eyes were soft and expressive, and there was a sweetness to her face that came alive when the sun glinted on her mahogany red coat.

She saw me.

My nose was pressed hard against the window screen, trying to get a better look.

She bent her head in a friendly feminine nod, and my heart started pounding and fluttering. For the life of me, I couldn't understand why.

The wagon pulled forward as Tom slowed, and in my eagerness to catch one last fleeting look, I pushed the screen a little too hard. . . .

I heard Annie's voice and felt Seth pulling my collar. "Judge, don fall. You haffa stay inside!"

I came back to earth and the couch as the station wagon drove out of sight.

Seth caught the flapping screen and fitted it back into its frame. "See something good, Judge?"

I wanted to tell him. Of all the family, he probably could have understood.

"We must have passed a meat market," Tom joked.

"Or a chocolate factory," Maggie volunteered.

As Tom picked up speed downhill, the wagon came into sight once more. I scrunched down on the couch. I had acted like an idiot, and it didn't bear repeating.

But Seth was watching. "Hey, would you look at that beautiful red dog!" He looked back at me and started grinning.

As if on cue, the Irish setter sat up and began watching our camper, her perky head stretching to see above the camper being pulled by her owner's car. We were now right behind her. I could see her, but I didn't think she could see me.

I felt so *foolish*.

"Would you look!" Kathleen shouted.

"She's a berry purty dog," Annie said, patting my ears. "But I like you bess, Judge."

Not even Annie's special attention could take my mind off that beautiful dog. Mind? Is that what I said? No, heart. My heart was making *patoompha* noises, and I was sure everyone heard.

"It's still quite a ways to our campsite, so we better pull in at this gas station, Tom," Maggie said. "They might not be open if we head out early tomorrow."

Fine. As far as I was concerned, Dream Dog should go to Hong Kong so I wouldn't embarrass myself again.

It was time to move to the back of the van.

I put my head against the bathroom wall. I didn't feel like talking.

The family respected that.

When they got off to stretch their legs at the gas station, I realized pouting wasn't the answer. I was hot, my throat was dry, and I figured I needed to stretch my legs, too.

Tom, Seth, Kathleen, and Maggie, with Maura on her hip, were inside the station looking for pennies for the gumball machine. Annie was on her way to the rest room around the side. I trotted over to wait for her.

When she headed back toward the camper, she didn't see me. She was too busy inspecting her clean fingernails. I noticed she left the water running—the door was wide open. Sticking my nose under that faucet might be just what I needed to cool off.

It wasn't such a hot idea.

The door that hadn't closed all the way behind Annie gave in to a gust of wind and slammed behind me. It had an automatic lock. There was no way for me to open it.

Well, they'd miss me before they pulled away, wouldn't they?

Despite the drink I had just had, my throat got drier.

I tried to bark, but the effort was muffled by my panic.

I thought I heard the sound of the camper pulling away from the pump.

Surely, after all I'd been through to come this far . . .

My heart felt like lead.

Then I saw the doorknob turn.

When it wouldn't open, the party knocked.

I answered with a good, loud bark.

I heard footsteps running away—very fast.

Hmmm. Barking was not the answer.

The trick must be to lie low. Maybe the next person would try the door, find it locked, and go for a key from the attendant.

It was my best chance.

I waited.

It wasn't a high-traffic gas station. Minutes passed. Miles had to be separating the O'Rileys from me already.

Finally, someone else tried the door.

Another knock.

This time I stayed still.

They waited a few minutes and knocked again.

When they left, I knew it was to get the key from the station office.

I heard the key.

I also heard a lot of complaining about "lock" and "law" and "premium time" or something like that.

I planned to just slip out when the door opened. I mean it was a ladies' room, and I was pretty embarrassed by the whole matter. But before I could ease out, the woman backed in, still shouting at the man with the key. She shut the door, removed her glasses, and stepped to the sink to clean them. She didn't look in my direction at all.

She was very pretty. She wore a tweed blazer with a crimson silk blouse, and her hair was slicked into a tight blond bun. Even with the high leather heels she wore, she was tiny. A matching briefcase—quite ultra and marked with brass initials—hung from the crook of her elbow.

She still hadn't noticed me.

She was drying those thick glasses. Bending down to set her briefcase on the floor, she met me nose to nose.

I was prepared to be friends until I heard, "*Eeeeeeeek!* Bear! Grizzly! *Eeeekk!*"

Bear? I'd heard of mistaken identity, but this was ridiculous. If she would just put those glasses back on . . . so I nudged her hand.

"He's attacking! Help!"

Lady, please!

She got so excited that when she tried to yank the door open, the knob came off in her hand.

I sat there, helpless, listening to a chorus of *eeeekks*.

People started gathering at the door. "Are you all right, lady?"

"It's those darn fires in northern Canada. They drive these beasts down this way."

"Stand back, we'll have to break it down."

"Joe, get on your CB. We may need help on this."

"I've got a rifle in my pickup."

Rifle?

Meanwhile, Pretty Lady, who still hadn't put her glasses back on, began using everything she'd ever learned about self-defense. She battered me with the briefcase, threw water in my face, found some hair spray, and aimed for my eyes. I could hardly see.

I opted for the only defense plan I could think of. I buried my head with my paws and prayed.

I heard more banging on the door.

"Stand back lady, we're coming in."

Maybe they were coming in, but I was going out. The instant that door burst from its hinges and landed on the floor, I took a flying leap.

I was running blindly, but I was out.

Pretty Lady, spurred by the reinforcements, took one parting shot with the hair spray. Her aim was bad, and little droplets of jasmine mist went floating toward the rescuers.

In the confusion, all anyone saw was a blur of fur.

I was circling the gas station, looking for a place to hide, when I saw the Kit camper getting a tire change in the gas station bay. The dog of my dreams had been watching the restroom fiasco. I stopped dead in my tracks, smelling for all the world like a Japanese flower garden. Mortified? I wanted to die.

The setter looked in the direction of the trash dumpster at the side of the station. I made myself move and parked my body behind it. When the posse of people after the "bear" came charging around the corner, the red dog confronted them, barking excitedly. Then she ran fifty feet ahead of them. In a perfect hunter's point, she straightened her back, her tail, and a forward leg, her eyes riveted on a thick grove of trees just past the station.

They bought it.

By now, thirteen people had joined the chase and went sailing to find the "wild bear."

Seconds later, a certain familiar camper pulled back into the gas station. When Tom stepped out, Dream Dog led him straight to me.

Tom wasn't exactly smiling as I dashed from behind the garbage bin into the camper.

But I still felt good.

She had saved me. That beautiful, gorgeous Irish setter had saved me.

I would probably never see her again, but my heart was pounding with gratitude.

Or was it something more?

# Chapter 12

It was still light when we pulled into our first campsite on a knob above a boat dock on the Yellow River. I couldn't imagine why someone had given a river a name like that. It was more brown than anything. After the unseasonable dryness, it looked like an overgrown creek, not a raging river. Still, the narrow waterway had some current, and Tom and Maggie delivered a full two-minute lecture on the dangers of playing too close to the water.

It took a while to get the camper set up—hooking up the water, lighting the gas pilots, raising the awning and antenna. While Seth helped Tom, Maggie went inside to feed Maura, and Kathleen and Annie took a walk. I followed along behind.

Annie brought a pail and shovel, and Kathleen brought a book. After exploring, we sat down under a huge oak tree. It was cool and shady, a welcome respite from the hot sun. A rowboat, with a pair of wet fisherman's boots, a pole, and a bait box, was pulled up on the bank.

There's something about campers—an honor system, I suppose—they never hesitate to leave valuables unguarded in the presence of other campers. I had noticed expensive lawn chairs, grills, and unlocked motor homes during our walk. The small-town thinking was refreshing. Everyone trusted everyone else.

"Don't go so close to the water, Annie," Kathleen was saying.

"But the ground is duzdy. I can't make duzdy mud pies. See?" Annie blew a handful of dust at Kathleen, but Kathleen ducked in time.

"Well, make 'duzdy' cereal, then," Kathleen said. "If you go back to the camper with muddy shoes, we'll both be in trouble."

Annie sat down on a root of the tree, her chin in her hands, and pouted.

I went to her side and rested my nose on her feet.

It was a good time to be friends.

Kathleen went back to her book.

We sat there for a while, listening to nothing in particular. Then, suddenly, a light must have gone on in Annie's head. She jumped up and whispered to me, "Well, she dinna say a'ting bout muddy pawz."

I knew I was being drawn into a plot.

Annie hooked the pail handle on my mouth. "Pease?"

How could I refuse?

So I played waterboy, and Annie made mud pies in earnest.

When Kathleen looked up, she laughed. "Annie! You little slavedriver! Poor Judge."

For some reason, that unsettled Annie, and she took the pail from my mouth.

I figured she'd had enough water, so I lay down to relax.

I was taking in the scenery, when I noticed a coppery figure at the top of a far hill—slim and proud and pretty.

It was *her!*

She was with a boy about Seth's age. She was doing some prim figure eights, gracefully, precisely, the boy leading her on a silver leash that glistened in the afternoon sun.

No question, she was blue-ribbon material.

I felt clumsy, fat, and unworthy.

Still, I couldn't keep my eyes off her.

I moved to a spot behind the tree so she wouldn't see me. Lucky for me, it was a *very* big tree. For a few minutes, I forgot all about Annie. Then I heard Kathleen squeal, "Annie, what are you doing in there?"

I ran out in time to see Annie standing up in the boat and dipping her pail over the side to get water. Her shoes and socks were on the root where she had been sitting before.

As if muddy shoes had been her only fear!

Kathleen panicked—the worst thing she could have done. She made a beeline for the boat, slipped in the mud, and landed, feet up and face down, in the bait box. There followed a scream that would have cracked glass.

"Worms! Tadpoles! Oh, *yukkk!* Ishy poohy yukky . . ."

Bugs and slimies were not Kathleen's favorite things. When she stood up to shake the crawlies from her braids, the movement shook the mooring of the boat loose, and it pulled free.

It was a step too late to stop the boat, but I couldn't just let them sail away.

I overreacted, too.

I took a flying leap. One paw landed in the bait box, one paw inside the unbuckled fishing boot. It was the best I could do or sink us all by not landing in the middle. My tail dipped in the water, but I caught Annie's sweatshirt in my teeth and tried to squish the escaping worms with the rest of me so Kathleen wouldn't leap overboard.

The setter and the boy were watching the whole thing. He started shouting, and she started barking—loudly.

So did we.

Tom and Maggie and Seth heard the screams and barks and came racing over, little Maura on Maggie's hip.

Campers came running from every direction to help.

Before I could get out of the fishing boat and shake the worms from my fur, someone started taking pictures.

That was my cue to take off. What I didn't need were memoirs.

I wandered down the river and found a shady spot with a high bank. It was such a clear day. If I stretched my paw far enough, I thought I could touch the horizon. Toward the north, I could see a smear of gray reaching toward the sky. It was smoke, surely, from those Canadian fires that had sparked in the June dryness. I knew they were miles away, but for a minute I thought I heard them crackle.

I spun around, and there she was, her delicate paws barely snapping the dry grass. Her legs and ears were wet, and she held Annie's visor cap in her mouth.

In the confusion, it must have fallen in the river, and she had rescued it. Again, I had reason to be grateful, but as I sat there staring at those dark eyes, I got lost in them.

She walked closer and dropped the visor at my feet, smiling.

I was sure I heard bells. No, chimes. No, a harp! Maybe all three. But as she started to walk away, I realized it was someone calling:

"Reeny, Reeny, where are you? We have work to do."

Reeny. The name was perfect. Reeny.

Reeny and Judge. Judge and Reeny.

What was I thinking? I sounded like Annie!

But then I watched her hair curling in the breeze. She touched her shoulder to mine and left.

At the very least, I had just fallen in like.

# Chapter 13

For the rest of our stay at the campsite, I didn't run into Reeny again, but I thought about her. I heard campfire talk about Toronto dog shows, and I was sure that's where she was headed. I didn't think I would ever see her again.

Probably.

We had a wonderful stay. We ate barbecued chops, thick and juicy, and roasted marshmallows. Afterward, in the quiet of candlelight, Tom read us a story.

He dedicated it to me, and you can guess why. It was "The Night the Bed Fell."

It took two days and nights to bring us to the Canadian border. Tom was in no hurry. The kids and Maggie took advantage of the leisurely pace to see the best of everything.

We saw the Indiana dunes. Seth took two dozen pictures, and Annie built two dozen sand castles.

We swam in Lake Michigan.

We fished in the Kankakee River and grilled steaks when we didn't catch anything.

We met lots of fine, friendly campers. One

man told Tom how he made this trip every year to bring his Afghan hound to the Toronto Dog Show.

I wondered if he knew Reeny.

We had stopped for lunch some miles south of Detroit when Maggie brought up the Canadian crossing.

"I can't make out this map, Tom. Once we go through Detroit, are we supposed to take the bridge or the tunnel?" Maggie was tracing routes in pencil on the atlas.

"I wanna take the bidge. Is it London Bidge?" Annie crawled into Maggie's lap.

"How far to Niagara Falls after we get across the border?" Kathleen was asking.

"Did Niagnes fall down with London Bidge? Maybe we oughta take that tullell." Annie looked very serious.

"Don't worry, Annie," Tom said, scooping her up and winging her toward the sky in one of those daddy lifts. "It's not London Bridge, and it won't fall down. It's very substantial. Niagara is a waterfall, but we'll be heading for Toronto first, then swing around Niagara and New York."

Toronto? The dog show place? Reeny?

"If we can find it," Maggie said, still studying the map. I can't make heads or tails out of this."

"Won't we need our birth certificates and the Judge's papers?" Seth asked.

"Right. Where did we put them?" Tom plopped Annie beside Maura, who was nestled in the crook of my elbow, discovering her hand.

"The birth certificates are in the glove compartment," Maggie answered. "Judge's papers are still in the pocket of my blue sweater."

Kathleen jumped up to head inside the camper. "I'll go get the Judge's stuff and put it with ours."

A funny kind of look passed between Tom and Seth. It made me uneasy.

"Your blue sweater? The one with the big ribbed collar?" Tom's voice was softer than usual.

"It's the only sweater I brought. You told me to pack light, remember?"

"I remember now," Tom said.

Seth looked as if he were going to be sick.

"Uh, Mom, I think maybe we goofed." Seth gulped his words.

Maggie finally looked up from the map. She saw the quiet panic in the faces of Tom and Seth.

Kathleen came charging out of the camper. "Mom, we have a problem." She was holding the blue sweater in one hand and a wadded mat of papers in the other.

"While you and Kathleen took Annie to the playground, we went to the laundromat . . ."

Tom didn't need to say more.

"Oh, Mom, does this mean we can't take the Judge?" Kathleen was nearly in tears.

Maggie took the wad of papers that had made a trip through the washer and dryer. She

PACE ARROW

unraveled them and spread them out. The writing was hopelessly smeared, and the paper was thinner than tissue.

There was a long silence. The longer it lasted, the bigger the lump got in my throat.

It was Tom who made the decision.

"If you could smuggle Judge seventy-five miles before I noticed him, we can smuggle him past the border guards." Tom was speaking so out of character, I could hardly believe it.

"You mean the Judge will be *contraband?*" Seth's mouth dropped.

"No. It won't be like that. After all, we have the papers, legible or not. But if we just don't parade him past, I think it will be easier," Tom explained.

"I don't know, Tom," Maggie said. "They make these laws for our protection."

"That's just it, Maggie. We know Judge is legally qualified to enter Canada—he's had all his inoculations. I'll bet even Sister Hermengilda would consider this a technicality and give us her blessing."

"Pease, Mom. Judge jus has to see Canaday." Annie was tearing up.

"Suppose, Maggie"—Tom held Maggie's hand—"suppose we put in a long-distance call to Dr. Baker and ask him to forward copies of the Judge's papers to the campground near Toronto. Then we smuggle Judge in now, knowing Dr. Baker's official papers will be waiting for us at the campground.

Maggie furrowed her brow, but she was weakening. I could tell.

"Mom, Dad's right. It won't be wrong. Our timing will just be off a bit," Kathleen pleaded.

"Most times those guards don't really check," Seth was saying. "The traffic gets bottled up if they board every camper."

"All right." Maggie finally consented. "But what if it doesn't work?"

The same thought had crossed my mind.

# Chapter 14

The morning of reckoning dawned bright and sunny, but my insides felt like thunderstorms. Tom and Seth took longer than usual putting out the fire and sanding the ashes. We had heard CB reports of new outbreaks of fires, and we couldn't be too cautious.

It gave more time for the butterflies to play games in my stomach. I couldn't even finish my bowl of milk.

Finally, we boarded.

"There are days, Judge, when I wish you were a goldfish," said Tom, folding me into the tub.

"It won't be for nine hours this time, big fella," Seth assured me.

"We're going to cover you with these dirty clothes as a camouflage," Maggie told me, shaking out a bag of laundry.

A sock with some kind of smelly powder landed on my nose. I couldn't move my paw to get it off. My nose was beginning to pucker. Annie saw it and pushed it back.

"Socks are for feet, Judge. And none of these are big nuf for you," she said.

This time, Tom tucked my tail in behind my hip without the benefit of the confining shower curtain tie that had tripped up my exit before.

"Now, remember, everybody, just act natural," Maggie said. She picked up a book, plopped herself down on the back couch, and began to read in earnest.

Except the book was titled *The Mechanical Engineering of a Pace Arrow,* and Maggie couldn't engineer the replacement of a light bulb.

Tom pulled the curtain and shooed the rest of the family into their seats.

He must have been pretty anxious to pull this hoax off because he forgot to do some of the must-dos of camping before we pulled away.

The television antenna caught in the branch of a big tree because he had forgotten to take it down first.

Delay.

The electrical connection he had forgotten to disconnect caught on a picnic bench. Fortunately, we heard it dragging behind us before the cord severed.

Another delay.

The steel entry step hit a garbage can because he forgot to pull it in.

Delay again.

Tom was so frustrated that he didn't bother

to stop at the dumping station to release the waste water.

Well, we'd be at another campsite before too long. So long as no one used a lot of water, it wasn't a problem.

That's when Kathleen, being her unusually efficient self, noticed that in all the excitement, no one had finished washing up the breakfast dishes.

While Tom made his way to the Canadian border, she washed and rinsed, humming and making soap designs.

Finally, she finished.

That's when I felt something cold and wet slipping under my chest.

The holding tank must have been full.

Shucks, wouldn't you know the surplus would back up into the tub, the nearest drain?

I was going to bark to get Tom's attention when I noticed that we had slowed down and were easing up to a customs booth. The lines were long, but it was too late to mention the water problem.

Maybe I could play the part of a canine sponge. My hair was long enough. So what if it felt positively awful?

I decided to endure.

The sock with the funny-smelling powder was one of the first things to become saturated. It stuck on my chest. I craned my neck to avoid the sharp scent.

I heard Tom open the window to talk to the

customs inspector. "Yes, we're all American citizens. Seth, hand me those papers, please. . . . More than twenty-four hours. . . . Just the cigarettes in my pocket."

It went on for seven minutes. I didn't know much about routine interrogation at the border, but this seemed to be lasting a little long. I could hear cars passing us in the other lanes, and I began to wonder if we had drawn one of those very thorough, very uptight inspection people.

And then I realized the inspector was coming aboard. Tom got out of the driver's seat and gave everyone a stern look that meant *Hold still and don't blow it.* He went to the main door to let the patrol guard in.

I didn't feel so good.

The cold water was taking its toll, and my joints were throbbing. The smell of that sock was an insult to my nostrils.

I shivered and pressed my nose against the Formica to stifle the sneeze that threatened.

I could see with only one eye; the other was covered with laundry. The man was half Tom's height but twice as wide. What he didn't have in hair, he made up for in grease on his overlong forehead.

He was chewing tobacco. It couldn't have been his first plug of the day, because evidence of an earlier supply had dribbled and dried on his shirt, a once blue button-down that had long since been relieved of its collar buttons. His pants were too big and too long. He wore a tight belt to hold them up, and he had double-cuffed the legs.

Tom shook his hand genuinely. "Have you been aboard these campers often?"

The man grunted. "I'm just a fill-in."

The Canadians must have been in a terrible bind to have resurrected this character.

"Well," Tom said with one wide gesture that took in the whole camper but kept his feet in their very firm position on the top step, "we have everything we need to enjoy your beautiful countryside."

The man was not put off by Tom's six feet, two inches blocking his way. He pushed past, leaving the print of a work boot on Tom's Adidas sneakers.

Kathleen was chewing her fingernails.

Annie looked as if she would cry any minute.

Maggie's frown deepened.

The man opened cubby holes and shook the animals in Maura's car bed—now, what do you suppose he thought he'd find? That started Maura whimpering. He opened the closets and headed toward the bathroom.

Seth jumped up. "Excuse me, it must have been something I ate." He ran for the bathroom first.

But the man didn't leave.

He waited for Seth to come out.

And the longer Seth took, the more suspicious he got.

Finally, Tom said, "Seth, you may as well hurry."

A discouraged Seth came out.

We all figured the jig was up.

The water was floating almost to my collar, and the sock floated up with it. This time, the smelly powder was just too close to ignore.

I was so doused and so cold . . .

The man was reaching for the shower curtain when it finally got me.

The gust that accompanied my *aachooo!* flung dirty sock, underwear, dish towels, and wet dog hair on one very surprised border guard.

A Saint Bernard sneeze is no wind in the willows.

# Chapter 15

From somewhere, the man had produced a whistle. A piercing screech brought border patrols racing to our camper.

Maura began to cry, hard. When Maggie jumped up to scoop her into her arms, the oily, squat man screamed, "Don't move or I'll shoot!"

He was only holding the whistle, but under the circumstances, we all froze.

Annie was yelling, "Nobody bedder hurt Judge Bejmin!"

Tom was trying to explain calmly in an atmosphere that belied calm. "You're not going to believe this, but . . ."

Kathleen was standing on the couch, waving the smeared papers. "He's legal, he really is."

And Seth was saying, "This time I really am going to be sick."

No one was paying attention to anyone else, so I decided to add my two cents' worth. I gave a very big *woof!* that drowned everyone else out.

It echoed through the camper and rivaled the *aachooo!* in getting attention.

Maggie threw herself in front of the tub to defend me. "Now, let's get this straight . . ."

The next thing I knew, we were all being marched past the lines of traffic to a tiny office near the far curb.

It was no Disney parade, but it drew its share of spectators.

I could have been a sideshow clown, considering my getup. My wet neck fur was curling and matted, and various items of drenched dirty clothes were plastered to my body. Something dragging from my tail kept clicking on the sidewalk, but I didn't dare turn around to look. Four security people were holding me by ropes attached to my collar.

In this state of utter humiliation, I caught a glimpse of a yellow station wagon in the last line directly in our path.

No . . . please . . . not this. With all the yellow station wagons in the world, don't let this be.

But it was.

Without lifting my head, I eased my eyes upward, and there she was—the mahogany fur, the soulful eyes—looking right at me.

I wanted to die.

I tried to hide behind the Kit camper, but the guards marched me forward till I was only a whisker away from the name on her collar.

Shandon Noreen.

Reeny.

Of course.

A young boy, the same one I had seen on the hill, started pointing at me and talking to the driver. The car's engine was turned off. Reeny leaned out the back window, barking softly, and the driver got out of the car and ran toward Tom.

"Reeny! Settle!" he yelled, and instantly Shandon Noreen sat and was quiet.

The station wagon driver reminded me of an Irish setter—sloping shoulders, lean, kind face—but with thin silver hair. "What's going on here?" he demanded, not of Tom but of the border guard who had started it all.

"Just doin' what I'm paid to do." The guard stuck his chest out and boasted about how he had apprehended this "mongrel" trying to sneak into Canada, probably with some dread disease.

Mongrel?

Disease?

The driver ignored the guard and walked directly over to me. He patted my head, smoothed his hand along my chest, and loosened the ropes around my neck. He was in no way afraid. He reminded me of those guys in the circus who stick their heads into a lion's mouth and never bat an eye.

I rewarded him with one of my biggest licks. He addressed Tom. "Sir, I can't imagine what problem you're having. This is no mongrel. This is a fine-looking purebred Saint Bernard . . ."

Reeny stretched her head out the window again to hear.

"... though I can't give him too many points for grooming this morning!" The tall man began to chuckle.

Rats.

Reeny pulled her head back in.

The tall man spoke again. "Why would you smuggle a well-cared-for dog into Canada? If you were coming for the dog show, you'd have to have brought his official papers. Besides, you don't exactly look like criminal types."

Tom explained my situation briefly. Kathleen waved the papers again.

"I'm Joe Curtis, Dr. Joe Curtis, and I've been a veterinarian for twenty-seven years. Suppose we put a call in to your vet right now. I'll sign some papers that will cover your Saint Bernard until he can forward the complete set of official papers." With that, he handed his car keys to the dumbstruck guard, directing him to move the wagon, and marched into the tiny office.

When Annie realized that things might be turning in our favor, she jumped on Seth's back, hoping for a piggyback ride.

"Roger, give Reeny a little exercise while you wait for me," Dr. Curtis called to the boy in the station wagon's front seat.

The guards holding the ropes didn't know what to do with me next. None of them wanted to be the first to let me loose, even though I was wearing my most docile face. Finally, Dr.

Curtis pointed his finger in the direction of a patch of lawn with an evergreen by the side of the road. The guards disposed of their charge—me—by hooking my rope to the little wire fence around the shrub.

Not too bright, those guys. The little fence wouldn't have held a Pekingese.

Annie got off Seth's back and moved over next to me. Everyone else crowded into the small office.

"Well, big fella, you're going to make it after all." Seth patted my head. "But you sure don't travel first class!"

Seth's laugh at his own joke was interrupted by "That's the dumbest excuse for a well-bred animal I've ever seen."

It was the boy called Roger. In one glance I could see he was arrogant and self-serving and had a mean streak. Worse, he was three inches taller than Seth and probably the same age.

"You must not know much about dogs, then. Your father is a much better judge of character," Seth said.

"He's not my father. He's my uncle. And I've won more showmanship awards with Reeny here than he has degrees." The skinny kid ran his fingers through his sun-bleached hair and openly smirked at me.

Poor Reeny, having a master like Roger. I was sure she deserved better.

Looking embarrassed, she came to my side. Imagine taking up with riffraff like me.

She smiled, and I was putty.

I backed into the wire fence.

Why couldn't I just once be Joe Cool?

Reeny pretended not to notice.

"Oh, yeah? Well, Judge here could be a big winner, too. We haven't shown him much, just local contests."

Local contests? Did he mean the block picnic when we lived in Rockford?

Seth was digging a hole for himself, and I could see it coming. But only one of my ears was listening. The other was leaning in Reeny's direction.

My adrenalin was overproducing. Maybe this was more than "like."

"Shown him? Ha! Who'd look? You don't know the first thing about it."

"Listen, I haven't had that many opportunities," said Seth. "Why, I'd show him tomorrow and match you any day!"

"How about Tuesday?"

"Huh?"

I should have been worried about this conversation, but I had other things on my mind. Deep, dark eyes, red hair kissed by the sun . . .

Kissed?

I was feeling awfully warm, in spite of my wet fur.

"You're going to Canada, right? And you're on vacation, so you've got time. Of course, you've heard of the Toronto Dog Show."

"Sure, of course. Who hasn't?" Seth was in the middle of such a bad lie that even Reeny started to sigh.

Annie began patting Reeny's head. "What's your dog's name?" she called to Roger.

"Reeny. . . . So how about it?"

"Hi, Reeny." Annie kissed Reeny's nose. "Wanna marry Judge?"

Annie, *pullease*. I felt warmer than ever.

"Well, there is the problem of the official papers we smeared." Seth was beginning to feel pressured.

Reeny stood a little closer, and my blood pressure went up twenty points.

The troop came out of the office. Good timing. There was handshaking all around. Seth and I were starting to relax when Roger opened his big mouth again.

"Well, see you Tuesday—if you don't lose your nerve!"

Tom looked puzzled. Maggie turned to face Seth. Seth looked nervous.

I felt very cold again.

Roger looked over at Dr. Curtis. "Unc, would you believe this dainty Saint is going to be competition for Reeny?"

Everyone was uncomfortable.

"Uh, Dad, we were just talking, and we had this idea. I mean, since we're going to Toronto and all . . ." Seth was practically whispering.

"Roger, get Reeny back in the wagon," Dr. Curtis said.

Roger snickered all the way back to the car.

"I do have some entry forms, and you can have them if you like. But you will need those official papers from your doctor." Dr. Curtis seemed to be trying to give us an honorable out.

Tom spoke up. "Thanks, Dr. Curtis. We'll take those forms and see how things work out." He kept watching Seth.

Dr. Curtis said softly, "Junior handling can be a wonderful experience for a dog and a young person, if you don't take winning too seriously."

"That setter really does look like a champion," Maggie said.

I couldn't agree more.

Roger came back with the entry form and official dog show rules. He snickered one last time at Seth, then gave a cutesy wink to Kathleen.

Kathleen blushed.

Seth gritted his teeth.

I prayed for deliverance.

Finally, Roger and Dr. Curtis pulled away, and we walked back to the camper. No one said a thing. Something was still clicking at the end of my tail.

When I got into the camper, Annie began to shout, "Oh, Judge, lookee!" And with the snap of a hook, she removed the item that had followed me with a click since my ungracious exit from the tub.

It was one of Maggie's bras.

That settled it.

I had to save face and shine in the dog show.

# Chapter 16

Maggie fixed hot cider with cinnamon sticks while Tom set up our campsite later that day.

"Why not?" Maggie kept asking. "We've known the Judge is special for some time. It will be a good experience."

"He has no knowledge of the details of showmanship, but I don't see why we can't give him a crash course," Tom added.

Crash course? I had never even made it through obedience school.

"These papers Dr. Curtis gave us make it pretty clear," Seth pointed out.

"And working dogs are never first to show, so he can watch the other dogs and learn a lot," Kathleen said.

"'Sides, Judge wans to see Reeny agin. She kin make him feel speshul. She likes him." Annie was sharing her cinnamon stick with me.

"Well," Maggie said, "if Dr. Baker gets those official papers here on time . . ."

"Let's do it, Mom," Seth said finally. "Let's give it our best shot."

"What do you say, Judge?" Maggie looked at me.

I could hardly swallow.

Maybe the official papers wouldn't come.

They didn't.

Twice a day Tom called ahead to the Toronto campsite, and twice a day they said, "No, Mr. O'Riley, we have received no mail for you."

The dry weather continued. Our overnight stops were much more crowded than we expected. Many campers had been pushed south by the rash of forest fires. Occasionally, a campsite would post an early curfew because wild animals were wandering south to escape the intense heat and smoke.

I was very glad I had come along. My spot under the awning kept me alert while the O'Rileys slept.

Most of my practicing for the dog show was early in the evening.

Seth was quite a teacher.

I was to be Novice A, exhibited by the owner or a member of the family—in our case, Seth. This would be a little easier than the Novice B class, which could include professional handlers.

I wasn't really used to a leash, but when Seth called for figure eights, I just pretended we were running through the apple trees at home.

When Seth said to stand for examination, I imagined Maura sleeping between my feet and held perfectly still.

I got used to the terms: forward, halt, about turn, halt, down your dog. Tom pretended to be the show judge and called the orders out.

Concentration was my biggest problem, especially on the long sit and the long down, when I had to stay in place for what seemed like forever until the "judge" gestured to the "handler" to release me.

But I thought of a certain Irish setter, and I tried harder.

When we finally arrived at our Toronto campsite, we were greeted by a marvelous Yogi Bear. He shook Annie's hand, and she hugged his knees. That fulfilled all Annie's dreams of Canadian bears.

We asked in person about the papers, but they had still not made it.

To the surprise of everyone, Maggie took it in stride. "We're going to the registration office that Dr. Curtis told us about and that's that. We'll call Dr. Baker and have him dictate the American Kennel club papers he has on file."

"But Mom, it has to be on their official stationery with their seal," Kathleen whined.

"Then we'll write it on the washed papers we have," Maggie said firmly.

"I don't know, Maggie," Tom began.

"Hey, let's try it!" Seth said. "We practiced so hard!"

"But the paper's so thin." Kathleen was still worried.

"Maybe they don't check really close." Tom was thinking out loud.

The picture of the border guard flashed in my mind.

I tried not to be sick.

"We're going. Right now," Maggie announced.

Maybe she was afraid of losing her nerve, too.

Maura started a real crying jag. A bad omen? But off we went.

Kathleen, Seth, and Maggie arranged the old papers on a cinnamon roll cardboard backing. They traced the lines of ancestry that formed the sire tree and the dam tree.

Tom parked near a pay telephone booth and before we approached the office, he made the call to Dr. Baker.

We all surrounded him, trying to hear.

"Yes, I realize this is an unusual situation. . . . It could be the fires or just slow mail, I don't know, really. . . . You will? . . . Yes, I'm ready. . . . Champion Zwinghov Xesbo V Gero's Wonna? You said Champion? O.K. . . . Just a minute, please. Can you spell that for me?"

Tom was having a tough time holding the phone, writing, spelling. Pretty soon we all took turns. Maura, who had calmed down with the clanking of coins in the phone, started crying again, and that added to the confusion. We ran out of change. Seth raced to a drugstore while Annie stalled the operator, and we held the call.

"Champion Golden Eagle V Jumbo?"

"Ma-Bob's Little Moe V Mighty Moe?"

"Mugs von Molly?"

In all, Tom deposited fourteen dollars and eighty-five cents. But every blank on the official form was filled in. For that outrageous price we learned two important things. One, my family was into weirdo names. Two, there were twenty-three champions in my past.

I wondered if Reeny would have been impressed.

Most of my life I had thought of myself as a superklutz, but maybe, maybe . . . well, we'd just wait and see.

At the bottom of the certified pedigree form, Maggie wrote: "I hereby certify that this pedigree is true and correct to the best of my knowledge and belief."

She signed her own name.

We all took a deep breath and paused long enough for a silent Hail Mary.

Then we opened the door under the REGISTRATION sign.

The lady in the office had blue hair. It wasn't just a pale silver-blue; it was honest-to-goodness blue. It matched the rhinestones in the frames of her glasses.

We all crowded around the little walnut desk with its neat baskets of papers and assorted supplies.

There was a good deal of *ahem*-ing, but she didn't look up.

So I barked.

She jumped about a foot out of her chair, but not one hair of her blue coiffure wisped.

"Yes?" she said, forcing a smile.

Tom spoke. "We're here to register our Saint Bernard for tomorrow's dog show."

"You should have done that yesterday," she said. "In Canada, we require a forty-eight-hour period to process."

"We have a special letter and form given to us by Dr. Curtis that should waive that preliminary filing," Maggie said.

"Dr. Curtis? *You* are friends of Dr. Curtis?" She slid her glasses down her nose and studied the seven of us more clearly.

Her tone of voice was insulting, but apparently *Dr. Curtis* was the magic word.

"Let me see the pedigree papers."

Maggie handed them to her.

Her nose wrinkled when she saw their ridiculous condition, but she couldn't deny that all the information and the AKC seal were intact.

"There will be a fifteen-dollar entry fee, and it will cost another dollar seventy-five for the nose print and tattoo."

Noseprint? Tattoo? *With a needle?* I hated suffering.

But then I figured Tom was suffering with all the expense, and he wasn't complaining.

I resolved to be stoic.

Kathleen finally said, "Tattoo?"

"Yes. Over there on the table are some small metal disks. You dip a disk in that blue indelible ink, then stamp a mark on your dog. You'll need the one for Working Dog." She pointed and Seth went over to find what we needed.

Whew. No needle.

Annie and I followed.

While Seth was inking the Working Dog disk, Annie started playing with the other disks. And while he was busy stamping my nose, she was inking the others and stamping my paw.

She probably qualified me to compete with Terriers, Pomeranians, and French Poodles.

Kathleen noticed what was going on, swallowed her panic, quietly removed Annie and me from the scene of the crime, and spent the next ten minutes puzzling how to clean my now-blue paw.

Finally, it was over. I was officially accepted.

The O'Rileys were jubilant, cheering and singing all the way back to the campsite.

But I didn't feel so jubilant. I felt scared.

What if I didn't live up to their Great Expectations?

# Chapter 17

We were all up early.

My grooming became a family affair that almost preempted breakfast. While Maggie assembled combs and brushes, Tom started the scrambled eggs, Kathleen warmed rolls in the microwave, and Seth began scrubbing my blue paw with scouring powder. When that didn't work, Annie brought the white shoe polish.

When we finally sat down to the eggs, we discovered an uninvited guest. A badger.

He came thumping up to the picnic table. He looked us all over, decided none of us was his type, and continued through the campground.

"I didn't know they were so brazen," Maggie commented.

"They usually aren't," Tom said. "But those forest fires have sent a lot of animals scrounging."

"Those fires must be closer than we've thought." Maggie looked worried. "Turn on the radio, Tom. We better keep posted."

While my sprucing was in full swing, the radio announcer chatted away. The fires were closer than we thought, all right, but the winds were coming from the southeast, so we were in no danger. It was sad to think of all those animals losing their homes.

After two hours of pampering, Maggie stepped back and looked me over. "Judge, you are absolutely *handsome!*"

I was embarrassed but proud. I wondered if Reeny would notice, or if she would even be there.

She was.

We arrived at the dog-show site early, along with one hundred and eleven assorted participants. Just looking at the competition made me queasy.

I saw a Russian sheepdog that I hoped I'd never meet in a dark alley. His hair was thick and reddish gray, and he had small hanging ears and a docked tail. I couldn't find his neck, he was so stocky.

A Pembroke Welsh corgi, white and sable, was running unleashed. A little girl about Annie's size in a pink dotted dress was chasing after it, yelling "Mischief Mary!"

Reeny and Roger were working out just behind the judges' stand, a long narrow L-shaped table covered with trophies, score cards, and ribbons. Another young man, probably fourteen, was putting an Afghan hound through her paces. The aloof, dignified Afghan had long, silky hair and almond eyes and seemed to be trying to outdo Reeny.

I barked to Reeny, but she didn't even look

my way. She had her mind on her work. She wasn't smiling, and the look she gave the Afghan was almost hostile.

I had never seen her like that.

I barked again, and this time she turned around, but her expression was definitely "Can't you see I'm busy!"

I was feeling less like champion blood.

A slow-moving basset hound with a collar that read MIGHTY MAUDE waddled over in my direction. Behind her was a Doberman pinscher. His tag said DARLING DERRICK. He looked alert and powerful, yet both of them paused to give me a friendly nod.

It was the first nice gesture from the competition. It helped some.

We stood in line so Seth could pick up his arm band. A silver bulldog stood behind us. No one could accuse him of being just another pretty face. I was feeling a little sorry for him until I noticed that after his handler picked up the materials, the bulldog was escorted back to a long black limousine. When their parking place got too sunny, the chauffeur placed goggles and a scarf on the dog, lifted him into a car seat by an open window, and drove a few hundred feet to shadier digs.

I wished Grammy's dachshund Henry could have seen that. Kathleen ran back to the camper for the camera. Henry, who fancied himself the greatest gift to the dog world, was going to get a souvenir.

When we got to the table, I put my chin on a

stack of score cards and surveyed the judges. All four men wore suits in spite of the heat. Some of the ladies wore Sunday finery, too. One rather plump woman with a delightful smile had on green paisley silk and she was talking to a slender, blonde . . . with her hair slicked in a bun, a tweed blazer, and a crimson blouse . . .

It was my turn to think *"Eeeek!"*

I didn't have to look for her briefcase to tell for sure. I remembered the smell of her hair spray. She was the lady from the gas station ladies' room.

I thought about running away. When she walked over to put on Seth's armband, I fully expected her to scream, *"Bear!"*

But nothing happened. She was wearing her glasses this time.

Seeing her didn't exactly help my case of butterflies. The great monarch migration was starting in my stomach.

When I heard the announcement to get into position, I saw the O'Rileys all staring at me. They looked so hopeful. I couldn't let them down.

I walked by Maura's stroller to get one last whisker pull for luck. Annie planted one of her Hollywood kisses on my ear; then Seth and I left for the participant's chair he had reserved. The O'Rileys sat several rows back, little Maura at the end in her umbrella stroller.

I couldn't even line up right.

I nearly stepped on a Yorkshire terrier with

braids on her ears and pink ribbons on her back.

We had a long wait. Some of the white shoe polish had brushed off, and a hint of blue peeked through.

Maura got restless and Annie began to fidget. Maggie, wanting to watch the show peacefully, gave Annie permission to push Maura to some shade. Annie found a spot a hundred feet away—farther than Maggie intended. If it had been any other event, I would have gone with them . . . but at least it was on a bit of a hill, just past the judges' table, where they could still see the show and we could still see them.

It seemed safe enough. But just in case, I would keep an eye on them.

By some strange twist of fate, Reeny and I were the last two dogs to perform. When the announcer called "Shandon Noreen," Roger whispered to Seth, "Prepare to get stomped, dumbhead!"

It made me mad. I expected Seth to answer smartly, but Seth didn't. Instead, he gave Roger a warm, cheerful smile and said, "We'll see." Not a bite of sarcasm, just pure politician.

Smart boy. I owed him a super show.

I nodded to Reeny to wish her luck, but she didn't smile back. To her, this was business.

Heel on Leash was the first event, and it was worth a possible thirty-five points.

I couldn't look at Reeny. I closed my eyes,

remembering her smile from the window of that yellow wagon . . . the good feeling . . . and I gave it my best.

The figure eights went smoothly. Seth's grip was confident. When we moved to the Stand for Examination, I became aware of something else.

Applause.

Not just Maggie and Tom and Kathleen and Annie, but perfect strangers cheering, "Nice goin'," "Good-lookin' big fella," and "Hey, would you look at that big dog work?"

It gave me the courage to glance at Reeny, but I knew even before I saw her face that she was not happy. Because the better I did . . .

When we paused before the Recall, I saw Roger frowning and Seth smiling. I also saw the scorekeeper hold up the card.

Reeny and I both had a perfect score!

On the next break, I looked for Annie. Old habits stick with you. She was standing under the tree looking straight up and shaking her finger.

At what?

It broke my concentration, and I lost two points in the Recall. But so did Reeny. Because she was watching me, not as a special friend, but as a rival. It was time for the Long Sit.

When I got in place, I saw Kathleen standing on her chair with a big sign: JUDGE, YOU CAN WIN!!!!!!!

I looked up the hill at Annie for more moral

support, but she was still shaking her hands at two black dogs on a tree limb.

Tree limb?

The judge signaled the end of the Long Sit, and forty points were added to my score. Reeny had only received thirty-eight.

The command was issued for the Long Down.

"Handlers, leave your dogs!"

I watched Seth walk to the other side of the ring.

Dogs? Up a tree?

I squinted to look at Annie again.

Those weren't dogs. They were bear cubs! They must have been frightened by the forest fires. And if they were cubs . . . then . . .

I saw the big mama bear stomping toward Maura's stroller and little Annie. Everyone else was watching the show.

We had several minutes to go on the Long Down, but I knew I couldn't wait.

I jumped up, barking, and charged across the judges' table. Out of the corner of my eye, I saw Pretty Lady faint dead away. I should have been so lucky the last time I met her.

I knew I was creating havoc, but the more confusion, the more likely the big bear would be frightened away.

Dogs and people took off in every direction. Darling Derrick must have flown in from somewhere, because he was right beside me. Mighty Maude tried to run *under* the judges' table, tripped over her ears, rolled *up* the hill, and stood guard by Maura's stroller. The Russian sheepdog circled to the back of the bear, snarling and cutting her off.

I wished he had consulted me on that move. All I wanted to do was chase her back to the forest long enough for everyone to leave safely.

Maggie and Tom pushed their way through the crowd. Tom picked up Annie, and Maggie plucked Maura from the stroller.

I heard a police siren and figured someone with a CB had radioed and lucked out with a nearby patrol.

But the big bear was ready to strike, and even a few minutes of fighting could be disastrous. What would a ranger do when he arrived? Shoot the big bear? Leave two orphaned cubs?

I looked at Derrick, and I felt as if I had known him all my life. We came to the same conclusion. He must have been a family dog, too.

We went to the tree. Standing on our back legs, we each grabbed a cub.

Slowly, carefully, we walked to within a foot of the big bear and gave her back her babies. The Russian sheepdog stepped aside to let her return to the sanctuary of the trees.

When the dust settled on the excitement, my eye caught a last glimpse of a rich auburn coat and a thin, pretty face on sloping shoulders.

Reeny had not budged from the Long Down. She had, under the most trying circumstances, not balked at Roger's command.

Her Best of Show blue ribbon was guaranteed. She would go home with honor, prestige, and a budding career.

I would go home with my family.

The last time I saw Reeny, she was smiling, that same gorgeous smile I once thought was only for me. She was posing by her trophy, and some man in a plaid sport coat was talking to Dr. Curtis about Reeny's endorsement of his dog food line.

Good for Reeny. She had her world, and I had mine.

When the rains continued, we headed back to Decatur. Our last truly beautiful sightseeing moment was at Niagara Falls—the mist and the sound were worth the trip. We crossed into New York and reversed our course. This time, it was few stops and lots of driving. Our memories were already rich.

The camper nosed its way into the driveway in the middle of the night. In the pitch-black, I could barely see the house. I wondered if the construction had been completed.

Maggie and Tom looked at the sleeping children and voted to let them stay in the camper till morning. Then they headed into the house. Just inside the door, they found a package. Maggie pulled off the brown wrapping and read:

For special dogs, there should be special awards.

Sincerely,
Dr. Joe Curtis

Tom pulled out a very official AKC stamped blue ribbon with gold letters that said:

BEST OF FAMILY—
JUDGE BENJAMIN O'RILEY

Maggie hooked it onto my collar, and I headed back to my sleeping spot under the awning.

Because of all the places in the whole world, that was where I wanted to be.

With my children.

Wherever that might take me.

## ABOUT THE AUTHOR

JUDITH WHITELOCK MCINERNEY grew up in the small town of Metropolis, Illinois, and started her writing career at age seven with the printing of her Brownie Troop minutes in the *Metropolis News*. Eventually she wrote her own column during high school, and went on to graduate from the College of Journalism at Marquette University in Milwaukee, Wisconsin. After marrying her college sweetheart, she had four children, who figure in this novel with their own lovable St. Bernard, Judge Benjamin, as the hero. Her children, three girls and a boy, range in age from kindergarten through high school and are sure to be part of the author's upcoming books. The McInerneys presently make their home in Decatur, Illinois.

## ABOUT THE ILLUSTRATOR

During his teen years, LESLIE MORRILL worked in a zoo, which sparked his interest in animal stories such as *Judge Benjamin: Superdog*. He developed his artistic talents at the Graduate School of the Museum of Fine Arts at Boston and the Cranbrook Academy in Michigan. After working as an assistant professor in a Pennsylvania college, he returned to Boston as a commercial artist and to illustrate books. Since then he has over 60 books to his credit and is currently writing his own picture book.